# The Buffalo Storm

BY KATHERINE APPLEGATE

ILLUSTRATED BY JAN ORMEROD

CLARION BOOKS · NEW YORK

Clarion Books
a Houghton Mifflin Company imprint
215 Park Avenue South, New York, NY 10003


The illustrations were executed in watercolor and pastel.
The text was set in 18-point Adobe Garamond.



www.clarionbooks.com

Printed in Singapore

*Library of Congress Cataloging-in-Publication Data*

Applegate, Katherine.
The buffalo storm / by Katherine Applegate ; illustrated by Jan Ormerod.
p. cm.
Summary: When Hallie and her parents join a wagon train to
Oregon and leave her grandmother behind, Hallie must learn to face
the storms that frighten her so, as well as other, newer fears, with
just her grandmother's quilt to comfort her.

ISBN-13: 978-0-618-53597-2
ISBN-10: 0-618-53597-7

[1. Overland journeys to the Pacific—Fiction. 2. Frontier and
pioneer life—West (U.S.)—Fiction. 3. Grandmothers—Fiction.
4. Fear—Fiction.] I. Ormerod, Jan, ill. II. Title.
PZ7.A6483Bu 2007
[E]—dc22
2006015661

TWP 10 9 8 7 6 5 4 3 2 1

For my parents, with love
—K.A.

To Bridget Strevens-Marzo
—J.O.

I was not afraid of anything
(except maybe storms).
I'd coaxed a wild-eyed colt to take a saddle,
and climbed the oak by my grandmother's barn
higher than all the boys,
cloud-catching high.
I was not afraid of anything,
so when my papa said, We're going west to Oregon,
I begged to drive the oxen team
across the endless prairie.

I couldn't say the truth of it,
not until the night before the wagon rolled,
when I helped my grandmother
put the barn to bed one last time—
my grandmother,
who could bake a cake or birth a calf or build a barn;
my grandmother,
who did not much like storms, either.
I'm not going to Oregon, I told her.
You need me here to pick the best berries
and name the new kittens
and help make a wish on the first firefly of summer.
You need me here when the storms come strong
and you are afraid—
when we are afraid, together.

I need you so, my grandmother said,
but your mama and papa need you more,
with the journey ahead and the new baby coming.
From her pocket she pulled out paper and envelopes,
a sharp-tipped pen, and a jar of night-blue ink.
Write it all down for me, Hallie, she said,
all the things I've heard tell of—
the prairie dogs clowning,
the coyotes making crazy music.
You'll see buffalo, child, too many to count.
What a gift to hear the earth rumble as they run!
I ran my fingers over paper
cool and smooth.

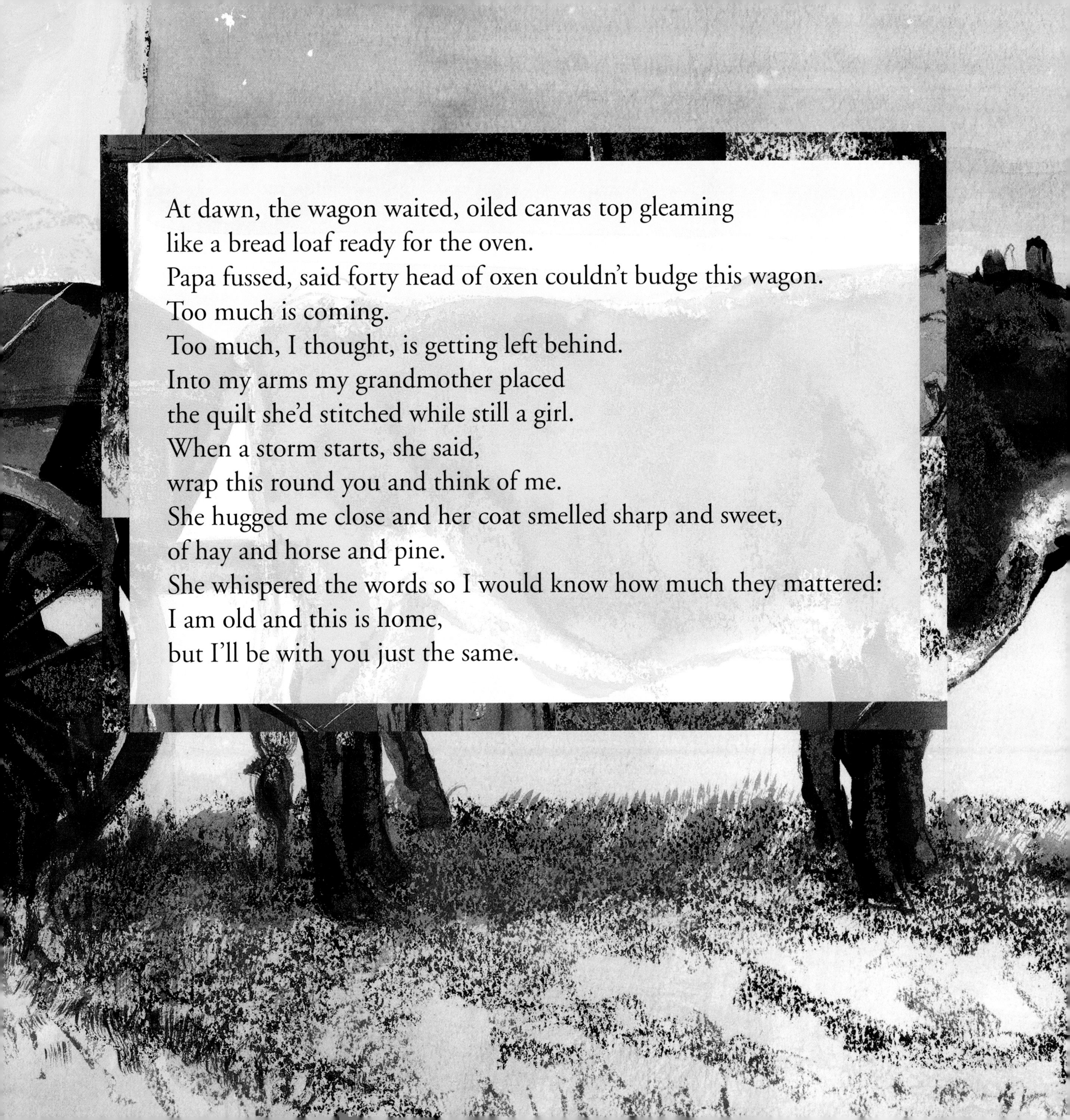

At dawn, the wagon waited, oiled canvas top gleaming
like a bread loaf ready for the oven.
Papa fussed, said forty head of oxen couldn't budge this wagon.
Too much is coming.
Too much, I thought, is getting left behind.
Into my arms my grandmother placed
the quilt she'd stitched while still a girl.
When a storm starts, she said,
wrap this round you and think of me.
She hugged me close and her coat smelled sharp and sweet,
of hay and horse and pine.
She whispered the words so I would know how much they mattered:
I am old and this is home,
but I'll be with you just the same.

We joined other wagons,
like beads slowly stringing.
Papa let me drive the team, though some said
I was too young and green, and a girl, to boot.
At night we circled. Fires spat and crackled,
children danced, babies drowsed.
Men boasted of the buffalo they would shoot
just to watch their great bodies fall.
Mama handed me the pen and the crisp, waiting paper.
Which way is home? I asked.
She pointed to my heart. There inside, she said,
there is home.
But I knew inside was just a hard place hurting.
I put the pen away.

The first storm came deep in the Nebraska night,
spun out of too much quiet.
Hail hurled down,
rain bounced off the stubborn earth.
I hid under my grandmother's quilt,
shaking fingers tracing the careful stitches.
Back home, she'd sing while the thunder rolled,
but now her voice was lost to me
as furious lightning split the sky
and the animals bellowed in fear.
I could not even hear myself cry.

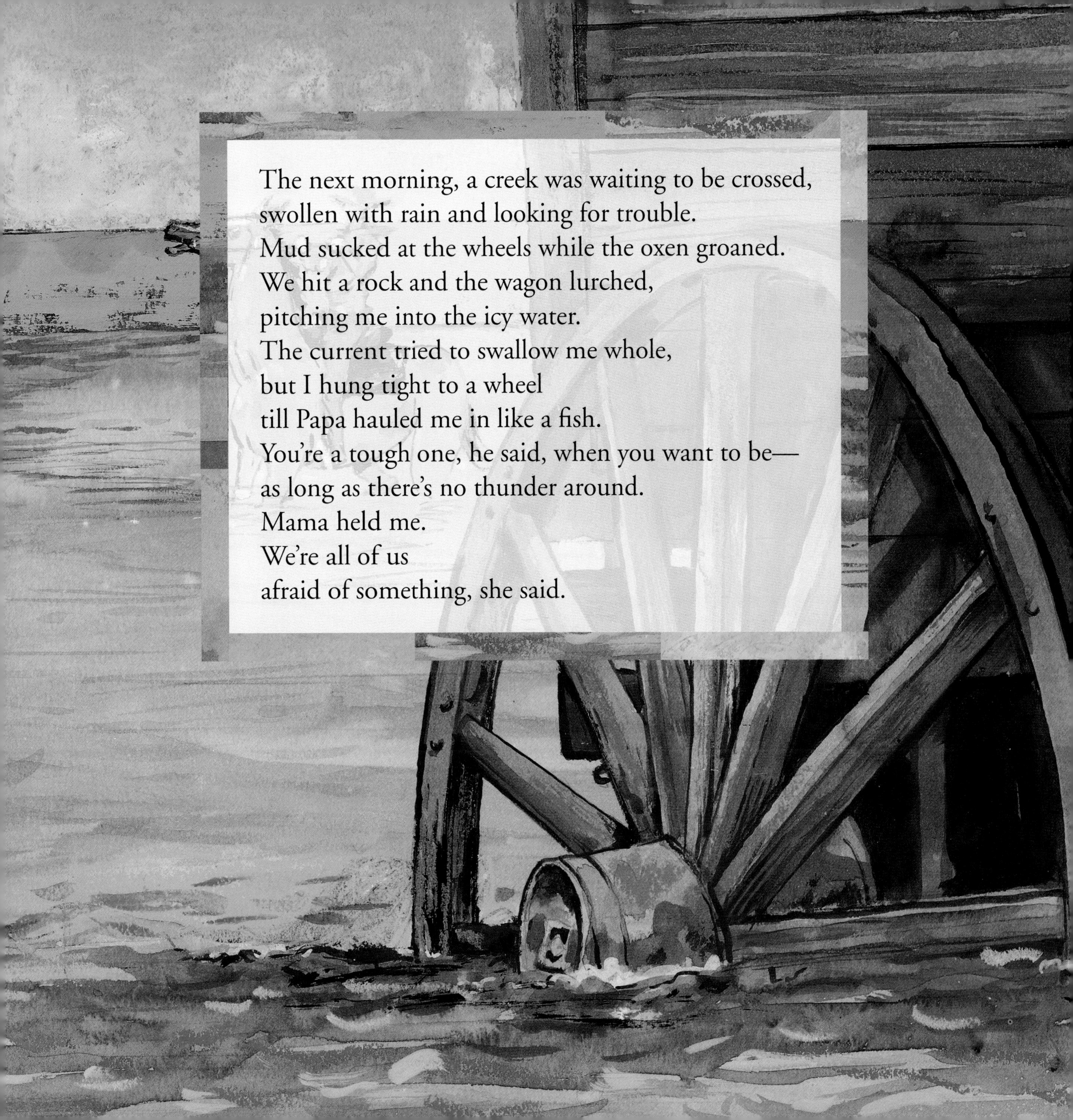

The next morning, a creek was waiting to be crossed,
swollen with rain and looking for trouble.
Mud sucked at the wheels while the oxen groaned.
We hit a rock and the wagon lurched,
pitching me into the icy water.
The current tried to swallow me whole,
but I hung tight to a wheel
till Papa hauled me in like a fish.
You're a tough one, he said, when you want to be—
as long as there's no thunder around.
Mama held me.
We're all of us
afraid of something, she said.

Weeks wove together and faded in the sun.
By the time we reached Wyoming,
the oxen hooves were bleeding
and my toes showed through my shoes.
One day during the nooning,
I searched for buffalo chips to feed the fire.
I rounded a sandstone ridge, and when I looked back,
the wagons had vanished in the dusty air.
I'm not afraid, I told a skittering lizard.
I couldn't say the truth of it,
not with the clouds so low and fierce.
A cry cut the stillness, and I spun around,
searching out the sound.

Past the ridge I saw her—
a little buffalo calf, red-gold, bawling,
leg wedged in a rocky place.
Her mother stomped and snorted,
riled as the black sky,
tail twirling like a lariat.
The calf cried again, and I knew what I had to do.
I was not afraid of anything
(except maybe those angry clouds).
She'd be no more trouble than a wild-eyed colt,
the one I'd tamed with my grandmother's help.

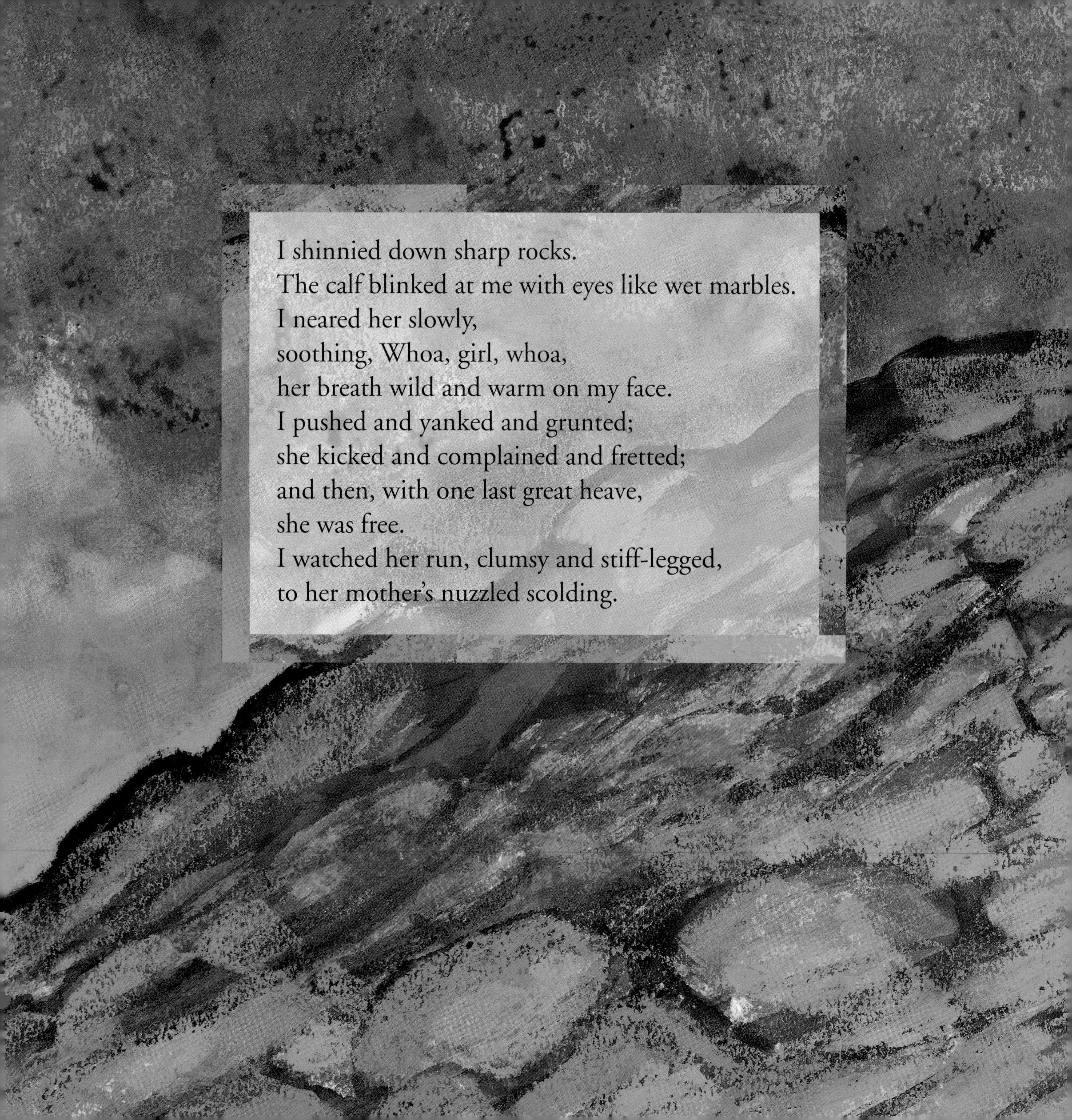

I shinnied down sharp rocks.
The calf blinked at me with eyes like wet marbles.
I neared her slowly,
soothing, Whoa, girl, whoa,
her breath wild and warm on my face.
I pushed and yanked and grunted;
she kicked and complained and fretted;
and then, with one last great heave,
she was free.
I watched her run, clumsy and stiff-legged,
to her mother's nuzzled scolding.

Suddenly, a noise like boulders breaking
shook the air,
and I knew a storm was coming,
bigger and louder than any I'd known,
a storm like no other.
Dust billowed, a thick brown fog.
I dropped to the dirt and covered my ears,
waiting for lightning to tear the sky,
trembling so hard that the earth itself
began to tremble, too,
and then I remembered my grandmother's words—
*What a gift to hear the earth rumble as they run!*
—and I knew.

Across the land the buffalo thundered,
huge and surly and crazed with life.
I stood, I stared,
I yelped with joy at the sight of it.
On and on, for miles and miles,
they moved like a black ocean surging,
an ocean without end.
Fine storm! I shouted,
and laughed just the way I knew
my grandmother would have laughed.
What a gift, I thought,
feeling my grandmother there,
there with me at last.

When finally they were gone,
the calf and her mother loping behind,
the air went silent as a prayer.
Dark clouds knotted in the sky
and blowing sand stung my cheeks,
but I kept walking.
When thunder rumbled, I didn't flinch or hide or cry.
It seemed harmless as a puppy's growl,
a tinny echo of something much grander.
At last, the wagons came into view
and then the rains began.

By the time we made Oregon,
my wool dress was worn and patched
as my grandmother's quilt.
The air tasted of autumn,
but the soil was deep and rich and waiting.
Hope grows big here, Papa said,
big like the trees.
I helped him make a simple cabin
to see the family through the winter.
A palace, Mama said.

I wrote my letter the day my sister was born.
Dear Grandmother, it read,
We named the baby Olympia—
my idea, after you.
When storms come, I will wrap her in your quilt
and hold her close,
just the way you used to hold me.
Oregon's a fine place,
with trees just right for climbing.
It's home now for me,
this new, wild place,
but I promise I'll be with you,
just the same.